INCH AND ROLY
Make a Wish

by Melissa Wiley
illustrated by Ag Jatkowska

READY-TO-READ

Simon Spotlight
New York London Toronto Sydney New Delhi

For Liza,
who makes wishes come true
—M. W.

For my Mum,
for all she does for me.
For Michal,
for all his love.
For Eddie,
for being my little miracle.
—A. J.

 SIMON SPOTLIGHT

An imprint of Simon & Schuster Children's Publishing Division
1230 Avenue of the Americas, New York, New York 10020
Text copyright © 2012 by Melissa Anne Peterson
Illustrations copyright © 2012 by Ag Jatkowska
For information about special discounts for bulk purchases, please contact Simon & Schuster Special
Sales at 1-866-506-1949 or business@simonandschuster.com.
The Simon & Schuster Speakers Bureau can bring authors to your live event. For more information or to
book an event contact the Simon & Schuster Speakers Bureau at 1-866-248-3049 or visit our website at
www.simonspeakers.com.
Manufactured in the United States of America 0712 LAK
First Edition
10 9 8 7 6 5 4 3 2 1
Library of Congress Cataloging-in-Publication Data
Wiley, Melissa.
Inch and Roly make a wish / by Melissa Wiley ; illustrated by Ag Jatkowska. — 1st ed.
p. cm. — (Ready-to-read)
Summary: Roly Poly, Inchworm, Dragonfly, and Beetle all feel bored one sleepy afternoon, until Roly
suggests they go to the wishing well to wish for something to do.
[1. Wishes—Fiction. 2. Insects—Fiction. 3. Worms—Fiction.] I. Jatkowska, Ag, ill. II. Title.
PZ7.W64814Inc 2012
[E]—dc23
2011043222
ISBN 978-1-4424-5276-3 (pbk)
ISBN 978-1-4424-5277-0 (hc)
ISBN 978-1-4424-5278-7 (eBook)

It was a sleepy afternoon.

The yard was still.

Roly Poly felt bored.

So did Inchworm.

So did Dragonfly.

So did Beetle.

"I wish we had something to do," said Inch.

"I have an idea," said Roly.
"We can go to the
wishing well.
We can wish for
something to do!"

"We will need a penny,"
said Dragonfly.

"Here is a penny," said Inch.
Inch was very good
at finding things in the dirt.

They walked and flew
to the wishing well.

"We only have one penny,"
said Beetle.
"We can only make
one wish."

"I have an idea," said Roly.
"I will wish for
three more wishes—
one for each of you!"

Roly rolled the penny
into the well.

She closed her eyes
and wished for
three more wishes.

"Look!" said Beetle.

"I found a four-leaf clover!"

"You can make a wish
on that," said Roly.
"The first wish!
My wishing-well wish
is coming true!"

"Look!" said Dragonfly.
"A dandelion."

"If you blow off all
the white seeds," said Inch,
"you get to make a wish."

Dragonfly fluttered
his wings.
The seeds blew away.
"I made a wish,"
he said.

"That is the second wish!"
said Roly.
"My wishing-well wish
is REALLY coming true."

It was getting late.
A star twinkled in the
pink sky.

"Look!" said Roly Poly.
"The first star.
Inchworm, now you can
make a wish.
It will be our third
wishing-well wish."

"But my wish already came true," said Inch. "It did?" asked Roly.

"Yes," said Inch.
"I wished for something
to do.
And we did do something!
We found wishes."

"Then I will wish upon the star," said Roly Poly. "I will wish for something to do—tomorrow!"